HELPING HANDS

Jennifer Moore-Mallinos/
Gustavo Mazali

NOT ALL HEROES
WEAR CAPES

WINDMILL
BOOKS ™

New York

Did you know that there are heroes all around us?
There are heroes in our neighborhoods, on the playground,
and even in our own homes. They are everywhere!

And guess what? None of the heroes I know wear capes or have superpowers or even know how to fly! They look just like you and me. They have two eyes, two ears, and walk on two feet, except for one hero I know: he has a tail and a wet black nose!

So how can a person *be* a hero if they can't fly or climb tall buildings or make things disappear? And how can a dog *be* a hero?

To me, being a hero means being brave and having the courage
to do what's right. It means being kind and helping others.
There are even heroes who help the environment!
What do you think it means to be a hero?

When I think about what it means to be a hero, I not only think of all of the people in the world who keep us healthy and safe, like police officers, firefighters, doctors, and our parents, but I also think about ordinary people like you and me.

One of my heroes is my brother, Ian. Every weekend, Ian volunteers at the local animal shelter. Not only does Ian make sure the homeless animals have a clean place to sleep, with clean water and lots of food, but he also makes sure that he gives them lots of love and attention.

Sometimes Ian will sit for hours
with a kitten or puppy on his lap,
gently petting them or even
brushing their tangled fur.
One time Ian spent so much time
playing in the pen with a litter of
kittens that he ended up falling
asleep with a bunch of kittens
curled up all around him.

Ian is a hero and he doesn't wear a cape or fly!
Ian is kind and thoughtful and tries hard to make
sure animals without a home feel safe and loved.
And if it weren't for Ian, I wouldn't have found
my other hero, Tucker.

Tucker is no ordinary hero! It just *so* happens that
Tucker has four legs, a fluffy tail, and a cold wet nose.
You're right! Tucker is my dog!

I know you're wondering how Tucker can be a hero. But don't forget, heroes come in all shapes and sizes. And just like other heroes, Tucker doesn't wear a cape or fly, but he is kind and he helps keep me safe every day!

Tucker is very special. He helps me get to school on time, he shows me my way through the hallways at school, and he even helps me cross the street! He's not only my best friend, but he also uses his eyes to help me see when I don't pay attention. Tucker is my guide dog!

There's another hero I know who is very brave and helps others by doing the right thing. Her name is Edison. We call her Eddie. Eddie doesn't wear a cape or fly, but she's my hero because even though she was really scared, she stood up to Brenda, the playground bully.

Everybody used to be so scared of Brenda.
Whenever Brenda came to the playground, all the
kids would run away. Then one day, when Brenda
was picking on one of the other kids, Eddie stood up
and told Brenda that it wasn't okay to be a bully and
that if she wanted to play with the rest of the kids
she needed to stop being mean!

I guess nobody had ever stood up to Brenda before because for the first time ever, Brenda didn't know what to say. Instead of yelling at Eddie, Brenda put her head down and walked away. The next day, Brenda came back to the playground and apologized for being so mean. She asked if she could play with us. Of course we all said yes. Brenda's been part of the group ever since then!

Finally, there's my friend, Nina. Nina loves to work with Mother Nature by planting trees and helping all kinds of animals stay safe. Nina doesn't wear a cape or fly but she's a hero! Without Nina, our forests would disappear and all the animals that live in the forests would not have a home. I couldn't imagine a world without trees, birds, and other animals!

There are so many things that make a hero. Whether you are a brother or a sister, a furry friend, or someone who is simply doing what they love the best, all heroes are thoughtful and caring. We can all be heroes! What can you do to be a hero?

Not All Heroes Wear Capes is a book that explores various qualities that can be considered heroic. Whether it is a simple act of kindness or having the courage to stand up for what you know is right, everybody has the ability to be a hero, even our children.

No matter your definition of what it means to be a hero, many of the qualities or characteristics that you consider heroic are often things that need to be taught through either role-modeling or intentional teaching.

We can inspire children to be their own hero and perhaps a hero for others by creating opportunities for them to develop these skills.

Here are some ideas to create a hero in all our children:

1. Encourage children to volunteer. Volunteering not only gives children the opportunity to experience what it feels like (the intrinsic satisfaction) to help others or to give back to their community in some way, but it also helps them to develop compassion. Having compassion for others is a quality that all heroes have!

2. Encourage children to look after the environment. Whether it is picking up garbage, planting a tree, or learning how to recycle, caring about the world around them teaches children respect.

Educator's Guide

3. Create a "Bully Patrol" where all children are part of the patrol and it is their responsibility to report bullying to an adult. Inspiring children to have the courage to stand up against something like bullying not only conveys a sense of camaraderie but it also empowers children by teaching them that they can make a difference.
4. Be the welcome wagon! Have children become active participants in welcoming new students to their school or new families to their neighborhood. This supports the qualities of being kind, caring, and thoughtful, all qualities that every hero should have.
5. Have a Hero Day! Ask children what they think it means to be a hero. Focus on the qualities and characteristics the child identifies. Choose one or two qualities and then ask the child what they can do to be a hero who reinforces those particular qualities.

6. Make your own hero cape that depicts what it means to be a hero. It can be words that describe a hero or it can be pictures that show the child doing things that inspire heroism.
7. Make a hero scrapbook of all the things the child did to be a hero.
8. Make a Hero Wall of Fame.

Through role-modeling, intentional teaching, or our everyday routines, we can inspire our children to be their own hero or a hero to others. Encouraging children to think outside of themselves is the first step in becoming a hero.

Be a child's hero and they will learn
how to be a hero themselves!

NOT ALL HEROES WEAR CAPES

Published in 2019 by **Windmill Books**,
an Imprint of Rosen Publishing
29 East 21st Street, New York, NY 10010

Book Design: Estudi Guasch, S.L.

Illustrations: Gustavo Mazali

Cataloging-in-Publication Data
Names: Moore-Mallinos, Jennifer. | Mazali, Gustavo, illustrator.
Title: Not all heroes wear capes / Jennifer Moore-Mallinos; illustrated by Gustavo Mazali.
Description: New York : Windmill Books, 2019. | Series: Helping hands
Identifiers: ISBN 9781538390665 (pbk.) | ISBN 9781508197331 (library bound) | ISBN 9781538390672 (6 pack)
Subjects: LCSH: Voluntarism--Juvenile fiction. | Community life--Juvenile fiction.
Classification: LCC PZ7.M788156 No 2019 | DDC [E]--dc23

Manufactured in the United States of America

CPSIA Compliance Information: Batch BW19WM: For Further Information
contact Rosen Publishing, New York, New York at 1-800-237-9932